STINKY and JINKS

My Hamster is a
PIRATE

BY DAVE LOWE

A TEMPLAR BOOK

First p   4 by Templar Publishing,

Deepdene

JF   www.templarco.c   UK

Illustrati

Illustrations by Mark Chambers
Design by Will Steele

Second edition

ISBN 978-1-84877-170-3

Printed and bound by CPI Group (UK) Ltd,
Croydon, CR0 4YY

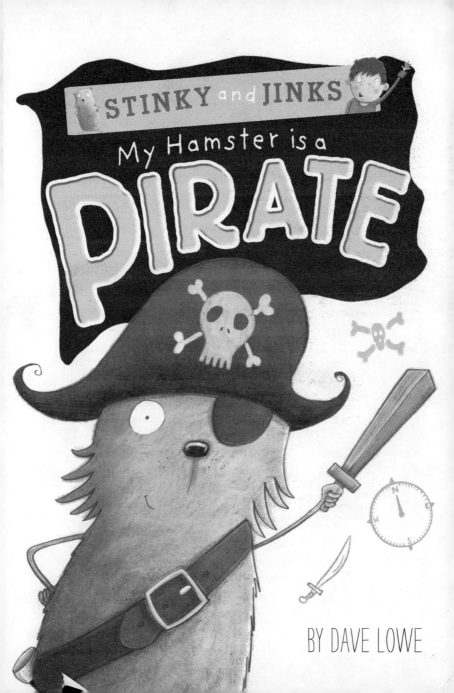

THE JINKS FAMILY
Me, Lucy, Mum, Dad and Stinky

To my brand-new nephew and niece,
James and Edith —
ahoy there, me hearties!

And with thanks to Miri and Rebecca
for all their ideas.

CHAPTER 1

We were having egg and chips when my dad coughed. At first I thought he might have got a chip stuck in his throat. But, no — he was coughing to get our attention.

"Your mum and I have got some great news," he said.

"Are we finally getting a pony?" squealed Lucy, my little sister.

"A baby brother?" I asked.

"No and no," my mum said, very quickly. "Absolutely not."

My dad said the next bit really slowly, leaving a big gap between each word to get us even more excited: "We. Are. Going. To…"

"The ballet?" gasped Lucy.

"The moon?" I said.

"The beach!" my dad announced. "For a holiday! Tomorrow!"

He grinned and waited for us to whoop with joy.

We didn't.

"But I'll miss my dance class," Lucy moaned.

She tap-danced a lot. A tap-tap-tapping sound came from her bedroom pretty much all the time. Living with Lucy was like living with a moody woodpecker.

"It's only for one week," my dad explained.

"And what about Delilah?" Lucy asked. Delilah was her cat. "What will we do with her?"

"She'll be fine," my mum said. "We're taking her to a cattery."

"What's a cattery?" asked Lucy.

"It's a place where they look after your cat while you're away. It's like a hotel for cats."

Lucy's eyes lit up.

"That sounds great," she said. "Can I stay there, instead of going on holiday with you?"

"It's for cats only," my dad explained, frowning. "Not for cats and people." He shook his head. "You know, most normal kids are actually excited about going on holiday. What about you, Ben? You're hardly jumping for joy, either."

"I am," I said. "Inside. It's just — what will we do about Stinky?"

Stinky was my pet hamster, and I was the only one who knew that he was a genius — a genius who got really bored when he was alone, even for one day.

"I didn't even think about Stinky," my dad admitted. "Can't we just put a whole carrot in his cage and leave him here?"

I shook my head and, luckily, my mum shook her head, too.

"And I guess we can't ask the neighbours to look after him," my dad added. He was right about that. We had the worst next-door neighbours in the world.

"Is there such a thing as a hamsterery?" Lucy asked.

"A what?" said my dad.

"A hamsterery. Like a cattery, but for hamsters."

My dad shook his head and chuckled.

"It's a very good idea, though — a holiday home for rodents. We could open a business and call it The Hamster Hotel. The Mouse House! The Guinea Pigsty! The Rattery!"

"You're not helping, Derek," my mum said, tutting.

"Can we take Stinky with us, Mum?" I said. "Dad? Please? He'll be no trouble."

My parents looked at each other. My dad shrugged.

"I suppose we'll have to," Mum said.

"Woo hoo!" I said and, straight after tea, rushed to tell Stinky the good news, but he didn't look nearly as excited as I'd hoped. In fact, he looked a bit grumpy.

"Come on, Stinky! A beach holiday! It'll be awesome! The sun on your fur! The sand between your tiny toes!"

"But I won't be on the beach," he snapped. "I'll be stuck indoors in this cage. And in any case, why would I want to go to the beach? There will be seagulls and crabs — neither of which will ever have seen a hamster before. They won't take long, however, to work out that I look like a very tasty meal indeed."

"But you were saying only yesterday how boring your life is, Stinky. A holiday might be full of adventure."

"Adventure?" he said with a sigh. "Like what, for example?"

"We could search for buried treasure. I'll take my bucket and spade, just in case."

He groaned.

"You've been watching too many movies, Ben. I expect that you think we'll discover a treasure map and 'X' will mark the spot."

"You never know," I said.

CHAPTER 2

Every time we arrive on holiday, the first thing that my mum does is have a cup of tea. The first thing that my dad does (after making my mum a cup of tea) is go out and get a local newspaper. "To get a flavour of the place," he says. "To see what's going on."

The first thing that Lucy and I usually do, however, is burst through the door of wherever we're staying and race each other to get the best bedroom. I'm nine and she's seven so I always win.

Not this time, though.

This time, Lucy ran in ahead of me, because I was carrying the cage with Stinky inside and if I dropped him, he would never let me forget it.

After I put the cage onto the bedside table of the smaller bedroom, I sat on the bed and waited for him to come out of his little house.

"Hey, Stinky," I said. "We're here."

When he finally poked his head out, he sniffed a lot and scrunched up his face. The sheet of newspaper that lined his cage was dotted with lots of little hamster poos.

"My cage needs cleaning out," he said.

"I did it only yesterday," I reminded him.

"I poo more when I'm nervous," he explained. "And, with your dad driving, there is a great deal to be nervous about. Unlike you, I wasn't wearing a seatbelt. And another thing —"

Stinky suddenly stopped talking because my dad himself came into the room, waving the local newspaper and grinning.

"Look what I've seen," my dad said, thrusting the paper into my hands.

I groaned.

FANCY DRESS FAMILY DISCO

PRIZE FOR THE BEST-DRESSED FAMILY

My mum was brilliant at making costumes, my dad loved competitions and Lucy adored dressing up. This was a terrible combination. Last year, for a birthday party, we'd gone as Goldilocks and the Three Bears. I was

Baby Bear, in a bear outfit with a nappy on. It was all very embarrassing.

"Come on, Ben," my dad said, ruffling my hair. "It'll be fun! And, speaking of fun, let's go to the beach! You've never really arrived at the seaside until you've dipped your toes into freezing cold water."

I got changed into my shorts and, before I left, I cleaned out the cage and used a fresh piece of my dad's newspaper to line it. This cheered Stinky up a little bit, at least.

When we came back from the beach,

three hours later, he was like a different hamster. He was pacing excitedly up and down his cage and, when I held out a couple of shells for him to inspect, he wasn't at all interested.

"Never mind shells, Ben," he said. "I have a feeling that there might be some actual treasure around here. Buried treasure."

I stared back at him in disbelief.

"Didn't someone tell me that people only found buried treasure in movies?"

"Well, that's what I thought. While you were playing in the sand, however, I did a little reading."

He tapped a paw onto the piece of newspaper that was under his feet, and I read the headline through the bars of his cage.

JEWEL THIEF'S NOTE IS STAR OF LOCAL EXHIBITION

"There once was a man," Stinky began, "by the name of Algernon Pickles, who lived very close to here, and who, twenty years ago, robbed a jeweller's in this very town. He stole eight pink diamonds, each of them as big as the nail on your little finger, but worth a great deal of money. The police caught him a few weeks later and sent him to jail. But they never found the diamonds."

"He must have sold them," I said, "before the police got him."

"Perhaps. But people were sure that he'd buried them and that he was waiting until he was released to go and dig them up. Here's the twist, though — he died suddenly in prison one day. He was killed in an unfortunate broccoli-related accident."

"Broccoli?" I said.
"I've always told
Mum it could
kill me!
I was right!"

**DANGER!
BROCCOLI**

"Anyway," Stinky continued, ignoring me, "when they were cleaning out his prison cell, they found a single piece of paper in his drawer."

"A treasure map!" I said. "I knew it!"

Stinky rolled his eyes.

"Of course it wasn't a treasure map. If it had been a treasure map, don't you think that someone would have read it and discovered the treasure by now?"

"I suppose so."

"On that small piece of paper were these words, in Algernon Pickles' handwriting: 'Crime never pays'. And that may well be true. But that is not what interests me. What

17

interests me is what was on the other side of the note. Something rather odd."

"Odd?"

"A shopping list."

I frowned.

"What's so strange about a shopping list? My mum and dad do them all the time."

"Do you think there are any shops in prison?" Stinky asked. I shrugged. "Of course there aren't," he said, impatiently. "Being in prison isn't like being on holiday, you know. Prisons are not nice places at all."

"Well, I know that now. Apparently, they even make you eat broccoli."

"So," said Stinky, "if there are no shops in jail, why on earth would Algernon Pickles have a shopping list?"

"Maybe he was writing down all the things he'd buy as soon as he got out."

"Perhaps. But the newspaper doesn't mention what was on the list. And, furthermore, he wasn't due to be released for a very long time. This is what I think: that the shopping list might be a code — a code which tells us where to find the diamonds. And you, Benjamin Jinks, need to go to the museum to find out."

CHAPTER 3

When we were all having breakfast the next morning, my dad asked us what we'd like to do for the day.

My mum said she was going to do a bit of work on the pirate costumes she was making for the fancy dress party, and then spend the rest of the day lying on the beach, reading a book and eating ice cream.

Lucy said she'd like to practise some new dance steps after breakfast, before cooling down with a swim in the sea.

"And you, Ben?" my dad asked.

"I want to go to the museum," I said.

My dad paused his spoonful of cornflakes just before it got to his mouth.

"The where?" he asked, frowning, as if he'd misheard.

"The museum."

Lucy giggled.

"There's an exhibition on, about local crime," I said.

My dad shook his head in disbelief.

"We're on holiday, Ben," he said. "An actual beach is just out there. The sea. The sun's shining. And you want to go to a museum?"

"Yes, please."

He sighed.

"Maybe tomorrow," he said. "If it rains."

My mum put down her cup of tea and frowned at my dad.

"We should be encouraging Ben," she told him. "He hardly ever wants to do anything educational."

"The *beach* is educational," said my dad. "All those pebbles. Shells. Crabs. It's nature, right on our very doorstep."

But then Mum gave Dad one of her special looks, and we all knew he'd be taking me.

In fact, my dad took me to the museum

straight after breakfast.

It was a small building and the sign on the door said that entry was free, which made my dad a tiny bit happier.

When we walked in, the grey-haired man who worked there — who'd been dozing in a chair — woke up with a start.

He was tall, wearing a name badge, and looked very surprised to see us.

Ted Slim rubbed his eyes and cleared his throat.

"Welcome," he said, in the whispery voice of people who spend a lot of time in libraries and museums. "We don't get many visitors on beautiful days like today. Most people are out relaxing on the beach."

"Of course they are," my dad said, looking at me and shaking his head. "Why wouldn't they be?"

"We came to see the crime exhibition, please," I said.

The museum only had one room, and Ted Slim pointed us in its direction.

"If you have any questions," he said, "I'll be right here."

And then he closed his eyes and went

back to sleep.

The first exhibit was an old fake banknote in a glass display case. Next was a newspaper report from a kidnapping one hundred years ago. After that was a 'Wanted' poster.

But it was the next exhibit that I'd come to see — The Mystery of the Missing Diamonds.

In a glass display case was the newspaper article from the day after the robbery. Next to that was the front page of the newspaper from a few weeks later. Then came a photo of Algernon Pickles himself and, finally, the note.

When my dad wandered off to look at something else, I tried to slide open the glass top of the cabinet, so I could flip the note and read what was on the back. But it was locked and there was no way to open it. I walked around the case, disappointed, looking for another way in.

There was a small round hole in the back of the case, just big enough to fit a ping-pong ball, but much too small for my hand.

My dad was getting fidgety, and we left soon after.

I hadn't given up hope of reading the shopping list, though. I had a plan.

The hole in the back of the case might have been too small for a hand. But it was just big enough for a hamster.

CHAPTER 4

"Absolutely not," Stinky said, as soon as I got back to our room and told him about my incredible plan.

"Oh, come on," I said. "You're clever, and clever people love museums."

"That may be correct," he sniffed, "but I'm not a person, in case you hadn't noticed. I'm a hamster. And clever hamsters keep well clear of museums.

Because, Ben, the only animals you will ever see in museums are ones that are stuffed. And I," he added, "most certainly do not want to be stuffed."

"I thought you'd be excited. It's an adventure! And in the newspaper it said that the diamonds are all five carat. You love carrots, Stinky."

He rolled his eyes.

"If you could spell properly," he said, "you'd know that it's an entirely different word. 'Carat' — C — A — R — A — T — means how big they are. A five carat diamond, for example, is..."

"As big as five carrots?"

He sighed.

"If I agree to go with you," he said, irritably, "will you stop annoying me right now, and leave me alone so I can have a nap? And get me five actual carrots?"

"Sure," I said, excitedly. "So you'll do it?"

He nodded, reluctantly.

"But first," I said, "I've got to get my dad to take me to the museum again, and he didn't even want to go the first time."

"I can't believe I'm going to do this, but — go and ask your dad if he'll take you to the museum if it rains tomorrow."

I did. My dad took one look out of the

window at the clear blue sky, grinned, and said, "Sure."

Then I went back to Stinky.

"Now what do I need to do?" I asked him.

"Nothing. It's going to rain tomorrow."

"How do you know?"

"It's instinctive, Ben. Animals are far more sensitive to changes in the weather than humans. Birds, for example, know that wet weather is coming a long time before people do. Dogs start barking well before a storm. And as for hamsters, we get this tingling sensation in our fur."

"Wow," I said. "Really?"

"No," he said, poking a paw at the sheet of newspaper lining his cage, "I just read tomorrow's weather forecast in the paper, right here."

10°C

CHAPTER 5

Stinky was right. It was pouring the next morning and Dad and me were dripping wet as we walked into the museum.

"You again?" Ted Slim whispered, rubbing his eyes. He'd been dozing in his chair again. "You're my best customers, you two."

"He's doing some kind of project," my dad said, pointing out the pen and the little pad of paper I was holding.

"Well, I'm here if you need me," Ted Slim said, with a yawn. "I'm just going to study the backs of my eyelids for a moment."

And then he rested his head on his hand and closed his eyes.

"Now, that's a job I'd like to have," my dad whispered to me. "Never a moment's excitement. Lots of time to have a nap or do the crossword. Speaking of which, I'll just be over here with the newspaper."

As my dad sat down and started on the crossword, I went straight to the note, hoping to solve my own puzzle.

Stinky was wriggling nervously in my pocket.

When we got to the back of the display case, I took him out and put him onto the palm of my hand.

But, now that he was here, I saw that the hole was pretty small, even for him. I sighed.

"Sorry, Stinky," I whispered sadly. "There's no way you'll squeeze…"

I hadn't even finished my sentence when Stinky thrust forward, wriggled and writhed and somehow managed to push his way into the hole. I'd forgotten just how good hamsters are at burrowing.

When he was halfway in, though, disaster struck. He got stuck. His bottom was still wiggling crazily, but he wasn't budging at all.

In a panic, I glanced at my dad. His head was still behind the newspaper. Ted Slim was still asleep. But Stinky was still stuck, no matter how much he struggled and squirmed. Not knowing what else to do, I gave his bottom a gentle push. Nothing happened. So I pushed it a bit harder and this time it worked.

Stinky tumbled clumsily inside the case and — when he got to his feet — he scampered over to the note. He quickly  nudged his nose underneath and managed to flip it over.

And there it was, in Algernon Pickles' own handwriting: the shopping list.

We both stared at it.

3 sausages
4 oranges
5 bread rolls
5 apples
4 pears
4 guavas
1 tomato
2 brussels sprouts
2 peaches
5 burgers

I sighed. I don't know what I'd been expecting, but this looked just like an ordinary shopping list to me. If there were any clues hidden in there, I couldn't see them.

Stinky, though, was jabbing a paw impatiently towards the pad of paper in my hand. At first I couldn't work out what he was saying and then I realised he wanted me to scribble down the list. So I did.

When I'd finished, I gave him the thumbs up, and then he flipped the note over and fixed it back down by walking on it.

But, just as I was about to help him get out, a man came into the room. He was old-ish and bald, carrying a dripping black umbrella, and he was shuffling right towards me. I felt all wobbly. What would happen if he discovered a hamster in the display case?

I mouthed the word 'hide' to Stinky. He glanced around nervously, searching for a hiding place. Then he scurried off to the newspaper front page, which was next to the note, and managed to wriggle under it, like it was a bedsheet.

He was only just in time, because the man stopped right next to me and peered into the display case. Like some bald men, he had lots of hair in other places to make up for having none on top of his head. His eyebrows were bushy. Tufts of hair sprouted out of his ears. Chest hair poked out of his collar.

I waited for him to move on and look at the other exhibits so that Stinky could come out, but the man was just staring at

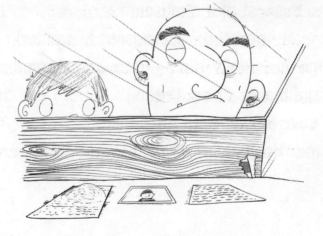

the note. Nothing else seemed to interest him. This was good, in a way, because it meant that he hadn't noticed the hamster-shaped lump under the newspaper page right beside it. But he kept on looking at the note and didn't move at all. Finally, he turned to me.

"There's lots of other things to see, you know, kid," he said, irritably, and gesturing to the rest of the museum.

I nodded nervously. I wanted to move, I really did — there was something frightening about the man — but I couldn't leave Stinky, even for a minute.

The man cracked his knuckles one by

one and whispered menacingly, "Beat it!"

I gulped and my legs went all wobbly. I looked at my dad — he glanced up from his paper but then went straight back to the crossword. As for Ted Slim, he was actually snoring now. But the bald man was glaring at me.

"Scram," he snarled. I edged away and pretended to look at another exhibit,

43

making sure I could still see him in the reflection of the glass.

He checked that no one was looking, and then took a paperclip out of his trouser pocket, stretched it out so it was like a piece of wire and — in one smooth movement — wiggled it into the lock on top of the glass case, twisted it, and then slid the glass open. Next, he lifted out the note, folded it, stuffed it into his pocket, slid the glass top shut and strolled out of the museum, twirling his umbrella.

CHAPTER 6

I wanted to yell, "Stop! Thief!" like they do in the movies, so that my dad would spring into action, but first I had to rescue Stinky.

The glass top of the display case was shut but now unlocked. I edged over to it, slid it open and whispered, "Stinky! Come out! Quick!"

He shrugged off the newspaper. I checked that no one was watching and then reached in. Stinky scurried over to my hand so I could lift him out. When he was safely in my pocket, I yelled, "Dad!"

My dad's head suddenly appeared

from behind the newspaper and Ted Slim woke up with a start.

"That man just stole something!" I shouted.

"Which man?" Ted Slim said, glancing around and leaping up from his chair. He rushed over to me, skidded to a stop and stared at the place where the note used to be. "My good goodness!" he exclaimed, his voice now nothing at all like a whisper. "The centrepiece of our exhibition! It's been pinched!"

My dad, meanwhile, had darted outside, but soon came back shaking his head.

"No sign of him," he announced. "On the plus side, though, the rain has stopped."

Ted Slim, looking suddenly pale, picked up the phone, and called the police.

Then we all stood there, waiting for them to come.

"Did you get a good look at him?" Ted Slim asked.

My dad shook his head.

"He was bald, that's all I noticed. An older bald bloke. Had an umbrella."

"I didn't get a really good look at him, either," Ted Slim admitted.

This was hardly surprising.

Then they both turned to me.

"I saw him," I said. "He had mean eyes. Bushy eyebrows. Hairy ears."

"Maybe you should draw a picture," my dad suggested, "for the police." He nodded at the notebook I was clutching.

"You know how rubbish I am at drawing, Dad."

"Being bad at something never stopped a Jinks," he said, proudly. "We always give everything a try, no matter how completely useless we are."

"Take a seat," said Ted Slim, eagerly offering me his chair and desk.

I sat down — very, very carefully, so I didn't squash Stinky. And this is what I drew:

I tore the picture out of the notebook and showed it to them.

"So," Ted Slim said, unimpressed, "we're looking for a man with a head shaped like a football, with one eye bigger than the other and whose ears are in the wrong place?"

"Good try, Son," my dad said, ruffling my hair. "Picasso wasn't very good at drawing faces, either. And his pictures sell for millions."

My picture must actually have been OK, though, because when the policewoman came, she listened to my story and took one look at the drawing before saying, "Oh, yes! It's Larry 'The Key' Skinner! I'd know that face anywhere. He's a burglar whose speciality is unpicking locks. No door — or museum display case, it would seem — is safe from Larry Skinner. But I thought he'd retired. Why he'd want to steal an old note is beyond me. And stealing a note with 'Crime never pays' on it seems very... What's the word?"

"Ironic," said Stinky, unable to stop himself. His voice was muffled by my pocket and, luckily, everyone thought it was me talking.

"Ironic, yes," said the policewoman.

My dad stared at me, his expression a mixture of stunned and impressed.

"Ironic," he repeated. "That's a fancy word, for you, Ben."

The policewoman went away to have a conversation into her walkie-talkie and when she came back she looked even more puzzled.

"It turns out that Larry Skinner was an associate of Algernon Pickles — the diamond thief himself."

Stinky wriggled in my pocket when he heard this.

"An associate?" I said to the policewoman. "What's that?"

"It means they committed crimes together," she explained.

My dad had finished his crossword and was getting impatient to go to the beach, and I knew that Stinky would be really eager to get out of my pocket.

"Can we go now?" I asked the policewoman.

She nodded and smiled.

"You'd make an excellent police officer one day, young man," she said. "You're very observant — unlike some other people I could mention."

My dad and Ted Slim both looked very sheepish indeed.

CHAPTER 7

Back at the holiday apartment, my mum was putting the final touches to our pirate costumes for tonight's fancy dress party, and Lucy was tap-dancing, as usual. But when my dad and me burst in, the sewing and the tapping stopped at once.

"You'll never guess what happened at the museum," my dad said, excitedly. "There was a crime. The police came!"

Lucy gasped and her eyes lit up.

"Did Ben get arrested?" she asked.

"No," said my dad, frowning at her. "Of course not."

She looked a bit disappointed.

"A man stole something," my dad continued, "and Ben here was a witness."

As my dad was telling them the story, I sneaked off to my room and popped Stinky back into his cage. He must have been really tense after spending so long in my pocket, because he went straight to his wheel and ran for ages.

Meanwhile, I put the pad of paper next to his cage and opened it to where

I'd scribbled the shopping list, so he could have a good look at it later.

As soon as he hopped off the wheel I asked, "Any clues?"

He glared at me.

"Give me a moment," he wheezed. "If you had been hiding from a robber and, moreover, spent an extremely long time in the pocket of a very fidgety boy, you would need time to recover, too."

So I sat on the bed and tried to give Stinky some thinking time.

But it was really hard to be patient when there was such an exciting mystery to solve.

"That man," I whispered, "Larry Skinner. He must think there's a clue in that note, too."

"Certainly," said Stinky. "Which means that we need to be quick, or else he'll find the diamonds before we do."

"But it looks just like an ordinary shopping list to me," I said.

Stinky shook his head.

"There's something rather odd about it," he said. "For instance, guavas — quite unusual fruit, don't you think? Especially all those years ago, when the note was written.

58

And two brussels sprouts. Doesn't that strike you as strange?"

"Even one brussels sprout," I agreed, "is one brussels sprout too many."

"No, Ben," he said with a sigh. "I mean, who would only buy a pair of sprouts? There is something most peculiar about the quantities."

"But what?"

"That's what I might be able to work out," he snapped, "if I had a bit of peace."

So I left him alone — for a few hours, because we went to the beach.

When I came back, Stinky had some news for me.

CHAPTER 8

"I know where the diamonds are!" Stinky exclaimed.

"Where?"

"Under a tree!"

I frowned at him.

"I know you haven't spent much time outdoors, Stinky, but there are thousands of trees around. Millions, probably!"

"The particular tree we are looking for, however, is in the shape of the letter V."

Perhaps Stinky had lost his mind. Maybe all that time in my pocket had made him crazy.

"It's in the shopping list," he said. "Have a look. What's the first item on there?"

"Three sausages," I said.

"Three sausages. Exactly. And what's the third letter of 'sausages'?"

I counted them out on my fingers.

"U," I said.

"Correct. So, get your pen and circle the U on the list. Now, 'four oranges' — what's the fourth letter of 'oranges'?"

"N?"

"Exactly — circle it, and circle the fifth letter of 'bread', and so on."

When I'd finished, I read the message that I'd circled.

"'Under V tree.' Brilliant!" I said. "But, hang on — that tree could be anywhere."

Stinky shook his head.

"Firstly," he said, "Algernon Pickles lived nearby, so it makes sense that he wouldn't bury them too far away. Moreover, he wouldn't have buried the diamonds in the dirt because someone would have noticed the disturbed ground and discovered them. With sand, however, you can bury something, smooth the sand back over and no one would ever know.

63

"Therefore, the diamonds will almost certainly be under a V-shaped tree, on the beach, and not far from here. All you need to do is find the tree."

"So, what are we waiting for?" I said.

"We?"

"Let's go out and find the tree-that-looks-like-a-V and dig up the treasure!"

Stinky shook his head.

"I've had more than enough excitement for today, thank you. I'm going to have myself a well-earned nap. It's your turn to do some of the work."

And then he waggled his bottom at me and disappeared into his little house.

So I went to see my mum, who was reading her book on the sofa.

"Can I go back to the beach for a bit, Mum?"

She looked up at me, putting her finger on the page so she wouldn't lose her place.

"The beach?" she said, frowning. "We've just been there, Ben."

"Just for a short while. Please."

She shook her head.

"We'll have to put on our costumes for the fancy dress disco, soon," she said. "And I know how long you take to get ready. You're slower than an elderly tortoise."

Then she went back to her book. I could tell that she was in a really exciting bit, and that gave me an idea.

"If I put my costume on right now," I said, "and leave you alone, can I pop to the beach for just a few minutes?"

Without looking up, she sighed, nodded and pointed to the costume on the table.

I got dressed in two minutes flat. There were ragged pirate trousers, a stripy shirt, an eye-patch, a bandana, a waistcoat and, finally, a plastic parrot to clip on to my shoulder.

I looked in the mirror and blushed.

I would feel incredibly stupid walking around outside like that, but I was desperate to find the diamonds before that horrible man got to them, and there was no time to lose. I dashed to my room to pick up my bucket and spade.

Stinky wasn't asleep yet. He peered at me from inside his house.

"If it isn't Short John Silver," he said with a chuckle.

"Come and help me find the diamonds, Stinky," I whispered. "Three eyes are better than one," I added, pointing to my eye-patch.

"I am not getting into your pocket again, if that's what you're thinking. Or into a bucket, for that matter."

"I've got a better idea. This parrot is hollow," I said, tapping it. "I can put you inside, and there's a little hole in its tummy you can see out of."

He stared at me for a while, and then he sighed, came out of his house and said, "OK."

I grinned.

"I must be crazy," he said.

CHAPTER 9

When you're pacing up and down the beach wearing a pirate costume with a plastic parrot on your shoulder, everyone thinks they can laugh at you. I was searching for the tree when I walked past a man and a woman who were sitting on deck chairs.

"Don't make me walk the plank, me hearty!" the man said in a pirate voice, grinning.

"Looking for buried treasure, matey?" joked the woman.

"I am, actually," I said, which made them both giggle. "You don't know where there's a V-shaped tree around here, do you?" I asked, but they both shook their heads and laughed some more.

It was Stinky who spotted the tree, and straight away I started running down the beach towards it.

It's not so easy, running on soft sand with a parrot balanced on your shoulder. Plus, Stinky was getting queasy.

"It's like your dad's driving all over again," he panted. "Being jiggled this way and that."

So I walked the rest of the way.

As soon as we reached the tree, I got down onto my hands and knees and started digging.

The plan (which Stinky had whispered into my ear as we were walking) was to dig a big circle around the tree, like I was making a deep moat. But it wasn't long before I realised that this would take me absolutely ages, especially as I only had a tiny plastic spade.

"Can't you help, Stinky? You're a great burrower. How about you dig in the sand for the treasure with me?"

"Certainly not," he said. "There might be crabs in there. Do you know what happens when crabs meet hamsters?"

"No."

"Me neither, but I have no intention of finding out. They have pincers, you know."

So I kept on digging by myself.

Stinky was whispering encouragement into my ear, which helped a bit, but digging for treasure was really hard work. After half an hour, I'd found three bottle tops and a crisp packet, but no diamonds at all. My pirate costume was all sweaty, my back was aching and I was exhausted.

"We should go back," said Stinky. "It's getting dark, your mum will be worried, and you'll be in an extremely large amount of trouble if you're late. We can always come back tomorrow."

"But what if Larry Skinner cracks the code and finds the diamonds before we come back? I feel like we're so close."

I started digging faster and faster — sand was flying everywhere — but, after a few more minutes, I stopped, exhausted. My whole body ached and Stinky was right — an angry Mum wasn't worth the risk, not for all the diamonds in the world.

"OK, Stinky," I said. "Let's…"

I didn't finish the sentence, because I'd spotted some dark green material poking out of the sand underneath me.

I quickly dug around it. It was a bag, no bigger than my hand.

I scooped my fingers under and pulled it out carefully.

It was tied at the top in a very tight triple knot, which I couldn't untie no matter how hard I tried.

"Let me help," said Stinky, so I took him out of the parrot, put him onto my palm and held the knot in front of him. He nibbled away at it with his sharp teeth and, in no time, he'd gnawed it open.

"Now put me back immediately," he said, "before a seagull spots me and thinks I'm dinner."

When I'd put him back inside the parrot, I looked around to make sure nobody was around, and then poured the contents of the bag into my hand.

Eight little pink diamonds, each of them glinting in the moonlight.

"Wow," I said. "Actual real-life treasure."

I put them carefully back into the bag, one by one.

But, in our excitement, neither of us had noticed someone arrive — someone who was now leaning on the tree, looking down at me.

A bald, angry someone.

CHAPTER 10

"You've got something that belongs to me, kid," Larry Skinner said in a slow, icy voice. "Give me that bag."

In one hand he had a garden spade and in the other a torch, which he shone into my eyes as I stood in the hole I'd dug.

"Wait—you're the kid from the museum," he said, frowning and leaning forward. "Who are you? Why are you dressed like a pirate? And how the devil did you know where to come to look for the diamonds?"

I was so frightened, I could hardly breathe, let alone speak.

"The contents of that bag you are clutching in that shaky hand of yours," he continued, "are mine."

I shook my head and this seemed to make him even angrier. His eyes bulged and his nostrils flared.

"I was personal friends with the gentleman who buried that bag," he said, leering horribly. "We worked together for a while. I opened doors for him. And when he went to prison, he told me that if anything happened to him, he'd leave a note with a secret code so I'd know exactly where

the diamonds were hidden.

"And then he went and died — death by broccoli, the very worst way to go. The problem for me was, I couldn't get hold of that note. Until now. And I've waited far too long to let a snotty little kid in a pirate costume get in the way. So,"— he glared at me and cracked his knuckles — "hand me that bag you're clutching. Then I can go home. And you won't get hurt."

I was still too scared to say anything.

Instead, it was my hamster who spoke. "Those diamonds simply do not belong to you, Skinner," he said.

Larry Skinner's eyes almost popped out of his head. He shone his torch at me, and then at the parrot on my shoulder.

"Who said that?"

"Me," said Stinky. "The parrot."

"That's a plastic bird!" Skinner jabbered. "How can it talk? And how does it know my name?" He shook his head. "I'm imagining things," he muttered to himself.

"The only thing that you are imagining," said Stinky, "is that you might get away with this."

Larry Skinner angrily jabbed his spade towards me.

"Do you want me to come in there, wring that parrot's birdy neck and whack you on your noggin? Because I'll do it. I'm not a violent man — not usually — but this is your very last chance, you little snake. Give. Me. That. Bag."

"Any ideas, Stinky?" I whispered to the parrot, my heart beating very fast.

"No," he said, sadly. "I think you better give him the diamonds."

So I climbed shakily out of the hole. Larry Skinner edged over to me.

"No funny business, kid. I've got a spade, and I'm not afraid to use it."

I gulped. I could see in his eyes that he wasn't joking.

Just as I was about to hand him the bag, though, I heard something behind me: quick footsteps and heavy breathing.

I looked over my shoulder.

There, in pirate costumes, were my family.

I'd never been so pleased to see them.

CHAPTER 11

My mum looked so angry she might explode. At first I thought she must be mad at me for being late, and she probably was, but it was Larry Skinner who she was glaring at.

"You just threatened my son," she said.

She'd painted a scar on her face and had a hook instead of a right hand. Even on good days, my mum was terrifying when she was angry. But right now, she was Larry Skinner's worst nightmare.

"What do you have to say for yourself?"
she went on, prodding her hook at him.
"Threatening a nine year-old boy, indeed.
You should be absolutely ashamed."

My dad pulled out his cutlass from its
holder and pointed it at Skinner. (It was a
plastic cutlass, but it looked real.)

Larry Skinner looked petrified.

"A whole pirate family," he muttered, looking around. "A talking plastic parrot. I must be in a very bad dream. Wake up!" he said to himself.

It was then that he started pinching himself.

"Owww!" he yelped. "Must do it harder. Wake up! Owwwww!"

This went on for a while, until he finally stopped pinching himself, took one last look at us, dropped his spade and torch, and ran off. He was really fast, for an old man, although he did lose balance a couple of times and crashed into the sand.

We all watched him run away.

"What did he mean, a talking parrot?" asked Lucy. I shrugged.

"You're late, Benjamin Jinks," my mum said, frowning.

This time I didn't shrug. I knew I was in trouble, and my mum isn't such a big fan of shrugging at the best of times.

"We were worried," she said. "We didn't know where you were. Luckily, a couple heading home from the beach pointed us in your direction."

"Sorry, Mum," I said. "I was going to come back. But then I found some treasure. And that man wanted to take it off me."

"Treasure?" my dad said, raising his eyebrows. I gave him the little green bag and he peered inside. "Diamonds!" he said, picking one out and studying it in the moonlight. "Nice ones, too."

"Diamonds?" Lucy squealed. "I've always wanted a real one! Can we keep them?"

My mum shook her head.

"There are many more important things in life than diamonds, Lucy," she said. "Besides, they're not ours. We're going to

90

take them to the police station, right away."

Then we marched off together, my mum leading the way.

The policeman on duty at the station was very surprised to see a family dressed as pirates, and even more surprised when my dad carefully opened the bag and poured the diamonds onto the counter in front of him.

"My son here dug them up on the beach," he said proudly.

The policeman was dumbstruck for a bit, but eventually he grinned and said, "It certainly makes a very pleasant change, pirates returning treasure, rather than stealing it." Then he shook his head, and added, "It never fails to surprise me, this job."

CHAPTER 12

Everyone enjoyed the Fancy Dress Disco. Well, everyone apart from Stinky.

Lucy had a great time because she was able to dance for hours.

My dad was over the moon because we won the fancy dress competition.

My mum was happy, too, because the prize was a huge box of chocolates. She preferred chocolates to diamonds, any day of the week.

I was feeling great because we'd solved another mystery. The jeweller had even given us a reward. Also, I was quite relieved that I hadn't been hit with a spade.

Only Stinky was grumpy, and I could understand why — after the police station, we'd gone straight to the disco and he'd had to stay inside the parrot the whole time. I think he was muttering complaints about the music into my ear most of the night, but luckily it was hard to hear him with all the noise.

He cheered up the next day, though.

I put five baby carrots in his cage for breakfast, and then let him nap for most of the day while we went to the beach.

When I got back to my room, I was holding a piece of newspaper.

"About time," he said. "My cage needs a thorough cleaning from top to bottom."

"I'm not cleaning your bottom," I said.

"Not *my* bottom," he snapped. "The bottom of my cage."

"Oh," I said.

So I cleaned his cage, but the fresh piece of newspaper that I put down inside it was a very special one. The headline said, '**Pirate Boy Uncovers Missing Diamonds**'.

Stinky grinned as he read it.

There was no mention of a hamster, of course. But Stinky rather liked it that way.

COMING SOON . . .

STINKY and JINKS

My Hamster is a
DETECTIVE

BY DAVE LOWE

Exclusive extract

ISBN 978-1-78370-031-8
Price £5.99

CHAPTER 1

It was my hamster who woke me up, as usual. His name was Stinky and he was like a small, furry alarm clock.

I wasn't a big fan of getting up so early, but I loved Saturdays because it meant I had two whole days to spend with Stinky. Even if he was pretty grumpy sometimes.

"What do you want to do today?" I asked him, sitting up sleepily. When he didn't answer, I said, "Let's have some kind of adventure!"

He glared at me through the bars of the cage.

"An *adventure*?" he spluttered. "How exactly do you propose I have an adventure, Ben, seeing how I'm stuck in *here* all day? Oh, perhaps I could go on my wheel for a fantastic running-around-but-getting-absolutely-nowhere adventure. Or maybe I could have an incredible taking-a-nap adventure in my tiny house. Or a fun poo-counting adventure — what wonderful adventures I could have here, inside this very cage!"

He could be really sarcastic, for a hamster.

"You don't *have* to stay in there," I said. "I can get you out whenever you like."

He shuddered.

"I am most certainly *not* coming out, not when that monster might be lurking around."

The 'monster' was Delilah, my little sister Lucy's ginger kitten, and she was actually very cute. The kitten, I mean, not Lucy.

"In that book I'm reading," I said, "the kids have adventures all the time. They're called the Secret Seven — six kids and a dog who are always solving mysteries. The dog helps a lot and, unlike you, *he* can't even *talk*."

"The dog in the story," said Stinky, "is he stuck inside a cage the whole time?"

"Of course not."

"Well, then," he said. "If he were, he

wouldn't be quite so helpful, would he?"

I groaned.

"Come on, Stinky. *We* could be a gang. Me and you. It would be fun. We could call ourselves the Secret Two."

"The Secret Two?" he said. "What's the big secret?"

"Well, nobody else knows that you're a genius, do they? *Or* that you can talk. So, that's *two* secrets, straight away."

"First of all," he said, sniffily, "a gang needs more than two. Two is a pair or a duo — certainly not a gang. Secondly, the Secret Two is a rather dull name. *The Secret Seven, The Famous Five* — they're *good*

names because the same letter starts both words. It's called 'alliteration'."

"'The Daring Duo'?" I suggested.

"Not bad," he said, "but what about *'The Tenacious Two'*?"

"That depends," I said, "on what 'tenacious' means."

"It means never giving up," he said.

"In that case, I love it. The Tenacious Two! Now all we need is a mystery to solve."

"How about the mystery of the nine-year-old boy who didn't clean out his hamster's cage for a whole week?"

"Very funny. How about the mystery of the hamster who pooed too much and was always moaning about everything?"

Just then, though, there was a loud knock at the front door, and suddenly we didn't need to find a mystery any more.

Because a mystery came to us.

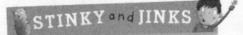